First published in 2010 in Great Britain by
Barrington Stoke Ltd
18 Walker Street, Edinburgh, EH3 7LP

www.barringtonstoke.co.uk

ISBN: 978-1-84299-895-3

Printed in Great Britain by Bell & Bain Ltd

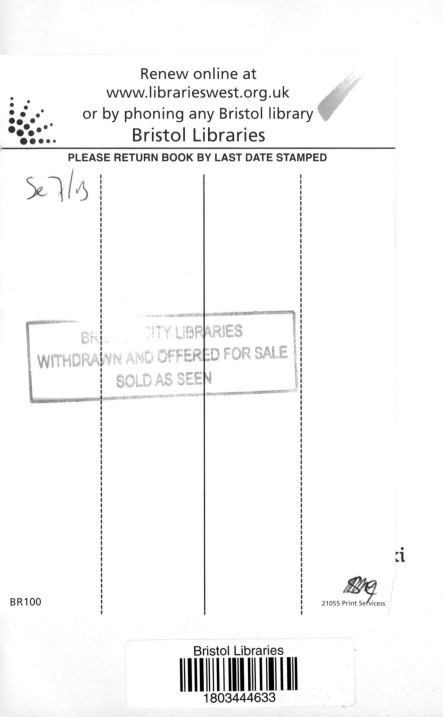

Contents

Chapter 1
The Fear

Jack stood on the side of the swimming pool and looked up at the diving platform. He wanted to throw up. It was hard to fake a smile. He knew everyone was looking at him; all his class mates, and the swimming coach.

The platform looked impossibly high, like it was about to topple over into the pool and squash everyone. It wasn't that he couldn't swim; that had never been the problem. He could swim for miles. For Jack, it was the height.

A mate called over, "Come on, Jack! You chicken or what?"

Jack tried to laugh and give a wave. It came out like a squeak and a shrug. He went to move forward, edge away from the pool towards the steps. It was more than a little difficult.

Then the swimming coach joined in. "Jack, you have to give it a go. You're a good swimmer – just get up there and do a jump, that's it. You'll be fine. Trust me."

Jack didn't trust him. Didn't trust anyone. Not when he was standing in front of a diving platform.

He took a step forward and felt the world spin. He wanted to sit down, anything but get on those metal steps.

The rest of the class started having a go at him, telling him to get a move on. The swimming coach tried to shut them up but it only made them worse.

For a moment, Jack just stood there looking up at the platform and at his mate making his way to the top, up the steep ladder. Everyone else enjoyed jumping off, couldn't wait to give it a go. He wanted to be a part of it.

Jack took some deep breaths. He tried to calm down, tell himself they were just steps, that it was just a diving platform, that jumping off would be more than fine, it would be brilliant. He could swim, couldn't he? Come on, Jack, sort yourself out! Do it!

But it didn't work. Heights had him by the neck and wouldn't let go. And the older he got, the harder they squeezed.

It was why he slept in a room downstairs at home, why he would never use a ladder. And it was all because of something that happened years ago.

Jack could feel everyone staring at him, their eyes burning into him. He felt hot, dizzy, trapped. The smell of the chlorine from the swimming pool stuck in the back of his throat and made him gag. All he wanted to do was get out, and fast.

Jack tried to block the memory that pushed him to this, that refused to let him go, but it pushed in to his mind, squeezed in between everything he was doing to keep himself calm. Deep breaths, Jack, deep breaths ...

He was seven again and it was a bright day, or at least that's how he remembered it. The weather wasn't important. It could've been raining for all it mattered.

The tree house used to be at the bottom of the garden. Jack had loved it ever since his dad had built it. The only way to get up was to use a ladder through the trap-door in the floor.

Jack would spend hours up there, on his own, or with mates. Since it had been built, he had made the tree house even more homely. Cushions covered the floor, pictures hung on the walls and an old wooden box held biscuits. Dad had put a few shelves in and these held books and comics and an old stereo, the one Dad had used in the garage that had got just a little bit covered in paint. But it still worked. Just.

Jack loved it. His friends thought it was great. And his dad wished he'd had something like it when he was a lad.

On that day, Jack had been up in the tree house all afternoon. It was warm and he'd been reading a new book from the library all about goblins and wizards and a magic stone. But he'd drifted off to sleep. He didn't remember exactly when, but he did remember waking up feeling groggy and hungry and thinking it was probably about tea time. So with a stretch and a yawn, he'd opened the trap-door.

Then it happened. Not like falling head first or tumbling out screaming. He just missed. Out went a foot, a hand, and where they should have found the steps of the ladder they found air.

Jack felt sick as the memory of that moment all those years ago thundered in to his head. The feeling of falling, of trying to grab at the ladder that seemed just out of reach, the fall which had lasted forever, and the landing.

His hand went to his left arm, just above his elbow. A lump stuck out where he'd broken the bone. Every day, it reminded him of that moment, the fall. It meant he could never escape the memory.

Jack breathed heavily, and took another look at the diving platform. Some of his class mates pushed past, laughed at him, called him names. And they weren't even the cool kids. They were just normal, like him, and that was a real kick in the teeth.

There was a yell from above. Jack looked up, saw one of his mates wave then jump, laughing all the way to the big splash at the bottom.

He couldn't do it. He just turned around and left as quickly as he could.

The swimming coach called after him and caught him at the door to the changing rooms.

"Come on, Jack, you've got to face up to it. Give it another shot. You'll be fine."

But Jack wasn't going to face up to it. Not today. Not ever. So he turned his back on the pool, got changed, and wished he was dead.

Later that day, after school and every step of the way home, Jack felt more and more useless. He was a let down, a chicken, a total wuss. The butt of every joke in the class. Everyone would be talking about him now behind his back. He hated it, but couldn't do anything about it. It made him so angry. All because of that one fall, all those years ago. How would he ever beat it?

Chapter 2
You Only Live Once

It was a bright Saturday morning. Jack was munching breakfast and watching TV. He was still thinking about the day before – the diving platform, the swimming pool, the sound of everyone laughing.

Jack picked up the remote control and flicked through the channels. He finished off his toast. Nothing on, just the local news. It was nearly over though; he could sit through it. Something he could watch would be on afterwards he was sure.

The picture on the TV screen changed to grass, blue sky, and the sound of an aeroplane. An old man was having his 70th birthday. He was dressed in a blue boiler suit, with a daft-looking skull cap strapped to his head, and he was wearing a harness. A man with crazy blonde hair and a wild grin was standing next to him.

"So," said the man behind the camera, "what are you doing here, Tom?"

Tom then said something about skydiving, that he thought it was about time he got over his fear of heights.

"I've always been scared of heights," he said. "Wish I'd done this years ago to be honest. You only live once, after all."

Then Tom and the man with the wild blonde hair turned from the camera and clambered on to a plane.

Jack watched as the plane took off.

The TV screen changed; they were inside the plane now. Tom's harness was clipped in to the harness of the crazy blonde bloke. They were standing at the plane door. The door was open.

The man's voice came over with, "Happy birthday, Tom – see you in 12,000 feet!"

Then Tom was gone.

Jack gasped. He couldn't believe Tom, a 70-year-old man, had just jumped from a plane. Was he mad? How would that stop his fear of heights? The man must be out of his mind.

The picture on the TV changed again. Tom was belly down, strapped on to the crazy blonde guy, and grinning like a mad man. His cheeks were shaking with the wind rushing past. All round them was blue sky.

Jack had never seen anything like it. He'd always thought skydiving was something only blokes in the army did, or people with too much money and not enough brains. But now he was watching an old bloke do it. And not only that, this man was scared of heights.

Jack watched as the crazy blonde bloke pulled the rip cord. He saw the huge, white parachute explode in the air. Next Tom was coming in to land, and then he landed on his backside. The smile on his face was ear-to-ear. "Best thing I've ever done," he said. "I can't believe it. I just can't believe it."

"So," asked the man, "how's your fear of heights now, Tom?"

Tom grinned. "What fear?" he said.

Jack switched off the TV. What he'd just seen, well, it didn't make sense. How could an old bloke do that, you know, jump out of a plane? It made the diving platform look easy. And it made Jack feel not just daft, but angry with himself.

If Tom can do it ...

A few moments later, Jack was on the internet. The skydiving centre he'd seen Tom jump with was quite close to his house. The cost of the jump – £150.

Jack knew he had that in the bank. He was saving up for a new mountain bike. What if he was to use it to do this? What if he followed Tom and tackled his fear of heights head on – by jumping from a plane?

There was no what if. Jack shouted for his parents and told them.

They couldn't believe it.

Neither could he.

At school the following week, Jack told a friend about the skydive. He told them it was a secret. It soon wasn't. By the end of the week, everyone in his class knew about it. And no one believed he would go through with it. Some even thought he was making it up. It made him want to go through with it even more. He wasn't going to chicken out. He was going to prove them all wrong.

Chapter 3
Terminal Velocity

The sky was filled with people falling. Jack had never seen anything like it. Against the blue sky the parachutes looked like bits of coloured paper, like confetti at a wedding, floating gently down. Only this confetti had people dangling from it, screaming their heads off, whooping and yelling.

Jack couldn't believe he was at a proper skydiving centre. The place was buzzing, filled with people from all walks of life.

"Jack?"

He turned. His mum and dad were smiling at him, though his mum looked a little worried.

"I'll be OK, Mum," said Jack, smiling.

He didn't tell her that inside, his heart was trying to rap its way out of his chest and that his gut was so twisted with fear he hadn't eaten since tea time the day before.

Jack walked over to the front desk in the centre and handed over the forms his parents had filled in.

"Great!" said the girl behind the desk.

Jack tried not to make it too obvious that he thought she was well fit.

"Just wait outside," said the girl. "Grab a drink, whatever. You'll be called in for your briefing later on. Enjoy!"

Jack said thanks and went with his parents to watch more people jumping.

Jack was sitting in an old aircraft hangar. An hour ago, he'd arrived at the free fall centre. Now he was a step closer to jumping from a plane at 12,000 feet.

He felt sick.

"Morning, everyone!" a voice said.

Jack looked up and came face-to-face with the instructor. He looked about 30. His energy was amazing. He smiled and bounced from foot to foot. Just seeing him fired everyone up for what they were there to do.

"I'm Ash, and this is how it's going to run ..."

Jack, and everyone else, leaned in.

"First I'll show you a film of a tandem jump. It'll give you an idea of what you're going to be doing later on. Then we'll run through the kit, then you'll be paired with the instructor you're jumping with. And that's it – next stop 120mph; terminal velocity!"

Jack's mind repeated the speed over and over. 120mph ... he couldn't believe it.

Ash switched on the TV. The screen fizzed in to life. For the next few minutes, everyone sat in stunned silence. The camera followed Ash and the group out on to a plane. They were all different ages, different backgrounds. Then they were up in the plane, the sound-track thumping. Then the door opened.

The film switched to a close up of a girl not much older than Jack. Jack thought he knew her but he couldn't work out where from. She was grinning. Then she was out of the plane. Flying.

I'm gonna be doing that, thought Jack.

The film stopped. Ash stood up and said, "How awesome is that, then?"

No one spoke. A few nervous giggles filled the air.

Ash held up a harness.

"This is the tandem rig you'll be clipped in to," he said. "But first, you need to remove any sharp objects or valuables – empty your pockets and put this on."

Ash and some of the other instructors handed out some old jump-suits.

"It'll protect your clothes and stop bits of clothing flapping in free fall," said Ash.

Once everyone was ready, Ash pulled out one of the group; a man who looked about 40. He set him up with the harness, then showed how everyone would be clipped to their instructor.

"It's pretty simple," said Ash. "When we hit 12,000 feet and are over the Drop Zone, you'll edge over to sit on the lip of the open door."

Jack was trying to focus, but all he could think about was the height; 12,000 feet … 12,000 feet … 12,000 feet …

"The exit position is simple," said Ash. "Just follow the commands: head back, legs up and arms crossed."

The man followed the commands.

"All this keeps your hands away from the plane, and gives the instructor more control," said Ash. "When you're out of the plane you'll arch your back, and have your legs between the instructor's. Easy!"

Jack wasn't so sure any of this was easy. He wanted to leave. He felt sick, and dizzy.

Ash went on.

"After exit, you'll be belly to Earth. It's a stunning feeling. Your instructor will release the drogue chute which is a small parachute that helps stabilise and slow you a little. You'll get a tap on your arm – then you need to put your arms out like this."

Ash showed what to do with the man he was clipped to.

"At 7,000 feet, you'll get another tap to cross your arms again. The canopy will be deployed at 6,000 and you'll then glide from about 5,000. Any questions?"

No one said a word.

"Good," said Ash. "All you then have to think about is the landing. At about 20 feet from the ground, your instructor will shout 'Feet up, knees up!' You'll probably land on your arse. And that's it – your first free fall!"

People started to chatter. Before he knew what he was doing, Jack was up and walking.

He got to the door just as the girl from the front desk came through.

"Hi!" she said. "Where you going?"

Jack fumbled his words, said nothing, smiled. She really was beautiful.

"Seen the film?"

Jack nodded. "Yeah."

"It was me," said the girl. "About two years ago now. I was terrified. Best thing I ever did, though. Now I can't stop!"

Jack was amazed. He was standing, chatting to someone hot, and it turns out she was once as frightened as he was now.

"You skydive, then?" he asked.

"Every week" said the girl. "Have a good jump, yeah? It's awesome!"

Jack watched the girl walk away.

Then he turned back to the group. His fear of heights wasn't going to beat him. Not this time. Not ever. And anyway, skydiving, it seemed, was a great way to meet girls ...

Chapter 4
No Turning Back

The plane looked like an old mini-bus with wings. It rattled and shook and didn't fill Jack with any confidence. But that wasn't going to stop him. Nothing would. Not now. He'd come too far to back out.

Jack was in his jump-suit and harness and had a really stupid-looking helmet on his head. Not that he cared. He was jumping out of a plane; fashion didn't seem that important.

"How you doing, Jack?"

It was his instructor. A small bloke called
Jez who it turned out was also in the army.
He was in the Royal Engineers parachute
display team. *At least I'm in safe hands*,
thought Jack as he turned and answered,
"Fine!"

Another skydiver was walking with them.
He had a camera on his helmet. Jack couldn't
believe Mum and Dad had paid the extra to
get the jump filmed. He was chuffed to bits.

As they walked to the plane, Jack was struck by what a beautiful day it was. The sky was bright, the sun blazing away. It was perfect.

For a few moments, he thought back to that last swimming session. Once again he saw the faces of his class mates, could hear them laughing at him and teasing him. Not just about being afraid of heights, but about the skydiving. None of them had believed he would go through with it. It made him upset. It made him angry. And it made him even more determined to see the jump through.

Jez climbed on board, and Jack followed. Jez sat down on the floor of the plane, and nodded to Jack to sit in between his legs. Jack felt Jez clip him in to his own harness, and tighten the straps. A strap was then clipped to Jez. He knew from what Jez had told him that this worked like a seat belt. It would be unclipped when they got to 1,000 feet.

The last of the group climbed in. It was loud inside and the engines began to rumble and squeal.

The pilot's voice fizzed through the speaker system. Moments later, the plane moved down the runway, bouncing along the way.

Jack realised in that moment that this was it. There was no turning back. A few weeks ago he was afraid of jumping from a diving platform. Now he was heading off to throw himself out of a plane at 12,000 feet. It seemed crazy. It was. It was also oddly exciting.

The plane turned, paused, accelerated. Jack felt himself pushed back in to Jez. Then the nose of the plane lifted, Jack's stomach disappeared and they were in the air.

Jack had never been in a plane before. He gazed out of the window as the Earth fell away below him. It didn't feel real at all. It was almost as though his brain would not take in what he was doing. He played it over and over in his mind, the fact he was doing a tandem skydive. He thought about how long they'd be in free fall – 45 seconds at 120mph. And he thought about the look on the faces of everyone at school when he told them about it.

Jack felt Jez double-check the harness, the clips, and tighten everything just that little bit more. Then he showed Jack his altimeter on his wrist, that told them how far away they were from the ground. They'd just risen above 8,000 feet.

4,000 feet to go, thought Jack.

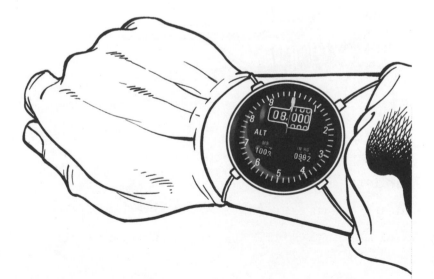

The pilot's voice came through. The instructors all gave a thumbs up, and grinned at all the first-timers. Jack watched as the one closest to the plane door pulled it open. Wind rushed in, gusting and battering around the inside of the plane.

Moments later, people were jumping. And they all seemed to be enjoying it.

Then it was his turn.

Jack felt Jez tap his arm. He then moved forward, and found himself sitting at the door, with his legs dangling. Between his feet he could see the Earth. He was so high, doing something so odd, that none of it felt real. The Earth looked beautiful, like a toy model. He could make out the criss-cross of roads, patchwork fields, houses, cars. It was almost as though if he just reached out, he could touch it – pick up a tree, or dip a finger into a lake.

Jack was suddenly aware that the camera man had climbed out. He gave Jack the thumbs up. Jack did his best smile back at him.

Then he heard Jez shout, "Head back! Legs up and arms crossed!"

They jumped.

Chapter 5
Wow!

Jack felt like he was in a washing machine as they tumbled from the plane. Earth and sky flipped in front of him. He had no idea what was up or what was down. He couldn't believe the sound of the air as they were falling. It screamed in his ears. And every time he took a breath, it was snatched away.

But he was smiling. Really, properly smiling. This was the best feeling in the world!

Jez steadied them and Jack felt him tap on his arm. He pulled his arms open. This was it! He was fully skydiving! Wow!

All thoughts of fear fizzled away as Jack looked around him. He was doing 120mph, racing down to Earth, but it didn't feel like he was moving at all. Everything looked so beautiful. And he felt so alive. It was such a high he wondered if he'd ever come down from it. He didn't think he'd ever want to.

They were two and a half miles up. No way!

The guy with the camera gave a thumbs up. Jack did the same. This was all on film! Brilliant!

Jez then sent them to spin right, then left, then right again. His cheeks were starting to hurt. Not just from the grin he couldn't tear from his face, but the wind. It ripped past, felt like it was trying to pull him to pieces.

Jack felt another tap on his arm, remembered the training, and crossed his arms. The canopy exploded above them and he felt like he was being ripped in half.

They slowed from 120mph to 10mph in less than ten seconds. Everything was quiet, totally silent, as they now drifted with the faint wind, down towards the Drop Zone.

"Enjoy it?"

Jack didn't know what to say. Words weren't good enough. He was still smiling. "Awesome ..." he said.

"Fancy trying to steer the canopy?"

"You serious?"

"Of course I am," said Jez. "It's easy. Here, take these."

Jack took hold of the yellow loops
attached to the steering lines of the canopy.

"Just tug gently left or right," said Jez.
"It's pretty simple."

Jack had a go – he couldn't believe he was
steering.

"The Drop Zone's that patch of ground over there," said Jez, pointing down. "Take us towards it. I need a rest."

"But I can't land," said Jack

"I'll do that bit," said Jez with a laugh.

For the next few minutes, Jack felt a freedom he never thought possible. The height was no longer a problem. He was flying, gliding on the air, steering them down to the ground. He felt on top of the world.

Jez took over. The ground rose to meet them. "Feet up! Knees up!"

Jack did what he was told. They glided in, sliding gently in to the soft grass on their backsides.

The camera man appeared, and filmed Jack getting unclipped by Jez, and then standing up. He did a high-five. Jack couldn't help himself; he leant back, punched the air, and yelled out, feeling the adrenaline racing through him.

Walking back with Jez, he spotted his parents. They waved, took photos. Mum looked like she'd been crying.

"He was brilliant," said Jez to Jack's dad. "He's a natural up there. I'd be happy to train him up."

Jack turned, amazed at what he'd heard. "Are you serious?"

"About skydiving I'm nothing else," grinned Jez. Jack looked at his dad, his mum.

"Well?" said Dad. "How was it?"

Jack could say only one thing: "Can I have another go?"

SKYDIVING – THE FACTS
SKYDIVING JARGON

Skydiving: Freefall parachuting.

Canopy: The name for the parachute used for skydiving.

Ripcord: The handle a skydiver pulls to open the canopy.

Tandem: Where a student is clipped to an instructor wearing a canopy that is able to carry two people.

Rig: A term used to describe the harness worn by a skydiver. The harness includes the canopy, the reserve parachute and the system that allows the skydiver to release it.

Drogue chute (say 'shoot'): In a tandem jump, a drogue chute is released shortly after exiting the aircraft to reduce the speed of descent. It is later used to pull out the main canopy.

Cutaway/Cut Away: The term given for when a canopy doesn't open and the skydiver breaks away from it to release the reserve canopy.

Altimeter: A device that tells a skydiver how far away they are from the ground. This helps them know when to open their canopy.

Drop Zone: Also known as the DZ. This is the landing area for a skydiver and is generally clearly marked.

Jump-suit: Overalls worn by skydivers.

Wingsuit: The wingsuit is a special type of jump-suit. It has fabric sewn between the legs and under the arms. This material helps a skydiver to glide through the air. They were first used in the 1930s, but were not very safe. In 1998 two skydivers created a new kind of wingsuit and it was the first to be offered to the general public. Some people are trying to work out how to land with only a wingsuit, without using a canopy.

Parachute jump: According to records, the first successful parachute jumps were carried out by Andre-Jacques Garnerin in 1797. He jumped from a hot-air balloon. Parachuting was first properly developed by the military to save aircrews from emergencies in flight. It was then later used to deliver soldiers to the battlefield. Parachuting was recognised as an international sport in 1951.

Safety: Parachuting and skydiving look dangerous. After all, who would really want to throw themselves from a plane? However, it is relatively safe and deaths are rare. Accidents tend to happen when a skydiver is performing unsafe moves or has made an error in judgement. Skydivers must carry two canopies, a main and a reserve. The reserve is regularly inspected and re-packed (whether used or not) by a qualified parachute rigger. Skydivers also use a device that will open the reserve canopy automatically if the main canopy fails. Also, skydivers are now wearing altimeters that tell you the height by sound as well as on a dial so you can hear as well as see how far away you are from the ground.

If jumping from a plane isn't seen as enough fun, skydivers have invented plenty of other ways to enjoy themselves:

Swooping: The skill of gliding across the ground or water at a very low altitude, often with feet very close to the ground.

Cross-Country: The skydiver will open their canopy immediately after jumping. The aim is to travel as much as possible while still in the air.

Night jumps: Require special training as well as equipment, including a lighted altimeter, a torch to check the canopy once it is opened and a light visible for three miles.

Stuff jumps: In these jumps, skydivers jump from rear door aircraft over an area where no one lives with an object, for example, a rubber raft, a bicycle, or even a motorcycle! Think what it feels like to fall through the air sitting in a dingy! The skydiver breaks off from the object at a certain height to deploy their canopy.

Fire-fighting jumps: Skydiving is sometimes the only way to reach a remote area and fight a fire. The people who do this are called smokejumpers. They are equipped with a parachute and fire-fighting gear. They go in to try and control the fire until other help arrives. They wear heavy padded clothing because they could land on a tree.

RECORD-BREAKING JUMPS

Longest skydive: Captain Joseph W. Kittinger jumped from a balloon at 84,700 feet on August 16, 1960. He fell for 4 minutes and 37 seconds before his parachute was deployed automatically. He reached a top speed of 614mph.

Biggest number of people in one freefall group: On the 8th February, 2006, in Thailand, 400 skydivers jumped from five *Hercules* aircraft and joined hands.

Most number of skydives: Don Kellner carried out his 34,000th skydive on the 13th July, 2003. Cheryl Stearns carried out her 15,560th skydive in August 2003. Cheryl also has the world record for most parachute jumps completed in 24 hours – 352.

EXTREME QUESTIONS FOR DAVID GATWARD

Have you ever done a skydive? What made you want to do it?

Yes – nine years ago. I've just always wanted to. It's the kind of thing I knew I'd always regret if I didn't at least give it a try. And it was my birthday!

Where did you do the jump?

In New Zealand, with my youngest brother, over Lake Taupo.

What was it like?

Utterly amazing. Sitting in the plane waiting for the jump was terrifying – looking out the door to the ground below. Then before you know it, you're out of the plane and falling! It didn't feel real. The view was amazing. When the canopy opened, the glide down to the ground was so quiet. It was like flying.

If you were going to do a 'stuff' jump, which object would you use?

A bike! I love the idea of riding out the back of a plane – how cool would that be?

Which famous person would you like to do a tandem jump with, and why?

Andy McNab, because he skydives, and I'm guessing knows what he's doing!

Have you ever done any other extreme sports?

I've spent my life doing sports like climbing, caving and canoeing. I never had any interest in football!

What advice would you give to someone thinking about doing a skydive?

Find a local Drop Zone and just do it! You have to be a certain age, and there are other things that you'll need to consider, but if you're already thinking about it, just get on with it – you'll never regret it!

Barrington Stoke would like to thank all its readers for commenting on the manuscript before publication and in particular:

Shane Baldwin

Suzanne Cleaton

Tammy-Jo Evans

Ellis Grieve

Carole Heywood

Mason Harry Steptoe

Jack Stray

Paige Tompkinson

Nicola Treadwell

Debbie Whitmore

Ashley Woolridge

Become a Consultant!

Would you like to be a consultant? Ask your parent, carer or teacher to contact us at the email address below – we'd love to hear from them! They can also find out more by visiting our website.

schools@barringtonstoke.co.uk
www.barringtonstoke.co.uk

Black Death
by
Martyn Beardsley

The year is 1348. When Will comes home from France, the Black Death arrives with him. The terrible illness starts killing people in his village, and those who are left think it's all Will's fault. Can Will and his sister escape the angry villagers ... and the Black Death itself?

Killer Clone
by
Steve Barlow and
Steve Skidmore

The Doctor's been shot. The killer's DNA is on the gun. But 30 identical clones all have that DNA.
They all say they didn't do it.
One of them is lying.
Who is the killer clone?

You can order these books directly from our website at
www.barringtonstoke.co.uk

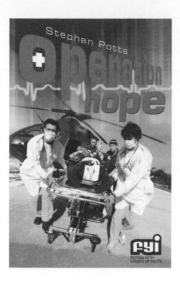

Operation Hope
by
Stephen Potts

David's kidneys don't work, so he feels sick all the time. He can never go on holiday and he's always tired. He's fed up.
A transplant would solve all his problems.
But whose kidney can he get? And will he get through the operation?

The Number 7 Shirt
by
Alan Gibbons

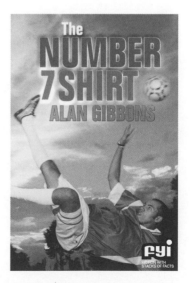

Football is Jimmy's life! When he gets into the Man U Academy, it's a dream come true – but he still has lots to learn. Lucky for him, he's got help ... his football heroes. They all have one thing in common – the Number 7 shirt. Will Jimmy win now he's got all the help he needs?

You can order these books directly from our website at
www.barringtonstoke.co.uk